CURIOUSITY LEADS
TO THE STARS
AF445699

Journey to ELYSIUM

I. The Remains of Babylon

Story, Layout and Concepts by
BONSART BOKEL

Art and Text by
YOHAN ALEXANDER

other art
Neurtron boar

RADIO RETROFUTURE

WHO'S ABSENT?
Is it You?

YOUR EXPERTISE IS REQUIRED TO SUPPORT THE ASSOCIATION ON THIS SPECIAL MISSION.
THIS IS NOT A DRAGOON OPERATION.
IT'S TOP SECRET. RA* DOESN'T INFORM THE HEADS OF STATE OF THIS ENTERPRISE.
IS THAT EVEN LEGAL?
COMMANDANT ANDREI ALECSANDRI, PROJECT BELLEROPHON SWISS OFFICER
*RA: THE INTERNATIONAL COMMITTEE ON RIFT RELATED ACTIVITIES
WILL YOU TAKE ON THE MISSION?
THAT IS THE ASSOCIATION FOR YOU, SON. THEY ONLY ACCEPT VOLUNTEERS. . .
DON'T WORRY, THE PROJECT* WILL NOT WITHHOLD YOUR PAY DURING YOUR LEAVE OF ABSENCE.
WHAT'S THE MISSION, SIR?
THIS ISN'T AN ORDER, SIR?
*: PROJECT IS SHORT FOR THE DRAGOON'S PROGRAM, PROJECT BELLEROPHON.
IS THAT A YES?
VERY WELL THEN. PACK YOUR GEAR. YOU'RE LEAVING AS SOON YOU'RE READY.

TELL, ME, YOUNG MAN--

WHERE DID YOU DEVELOP YOUR ABILITIES AS A COMMUNICATIONS OFFICER?
ORIGINALLY, THE DUTCH INDIAN ARMY. WE WERE EARLY ADOPTERS OF WIRELESS TELEGRAPHS. IT'S WHY THE PROJECT RECRUITED ME.

THE KNIL? I CAN IMAGINE.
SPEAKING OF WHICH, WHAT IS THIS OPERATION WE ARE EMBARKING ON?

WE SHOULD BE ARRIVING ANY MOMENT NOW.
ARRIVING WH--

SOME WEEKS EARLIER,
THE ATLANTIC, SOMEWHERE.

MERDE.
CLAN

WHO'S THE GIRL?
THE ASSOCIATION'S 7TH CHAIRMAN, AS I UNDERSTAND IT ...

BUT SHE'S A CHILD, DRESSED AS JEAN PAUL'S GRANDPA AT WATERLOO.
OUI, IT'S TRUE. IT'S A VERY SIMILAR UNIFORM.

QUEL ÉTAIT LE NOM DE VOTRE GRAND-PÈRE, SOLDAT?

JEAN PAUL GARVILLE, 4TH GRENADIERS.
VIEILLE GARDE, THE 4TH WAS AT GENAPPE, WAS IT NOT?
AH, OUI, YOU ARE VERY KNOWLEDGE-ABLE.

IT WAS OUR LAST STAND.

I GOT A VISUAL ON OUR DESTINATION.
TAKE AN EVASIVE APPROACH. THEY HAVE SEVERAL MACHINE GUN POSITIONS.

S- MADAME . . .
I WAS NOT INFORMED OF ANY HOSTILES.

SIR, IS FINE... AS FOR THE HOSTILES. THEY ACTUALLY WEREN'T THAT ENTHUSED WHEN WE ANNOUNCED OUR ARRIVAL. SO, JUST IN CASE, EVASIVE MANEUVERS.
UH, RIGHT . . .
PICKING AN EVASIVE COURSE... JUST IN CASE.

ARE YOU EXPECTING RESISTANCE, CHAIRMAN? THAT PLATFORM SURE DOESN'T LOOK LIKE FREETOWN.

I AM CERTAIN IT'S NOTHING THE ELITE DRAGOONS CAN'T HANDLE, SOLDAT.

THERE IS NOBODY HERE, CHAIRMAN!
I WASN'T EXPECTING A WELCOME! WE'LL HEAD STRAIGHT FOR THE DOME.
WHO STILL LIVES HERE?
DON'T WORRY. THE INHABITANTS ARE RECLUSES IN VOLUNTARY EXILE.
IT'S A MIRACLE THEY MANAGED TO HOLD OUT FOR THIS LONG.

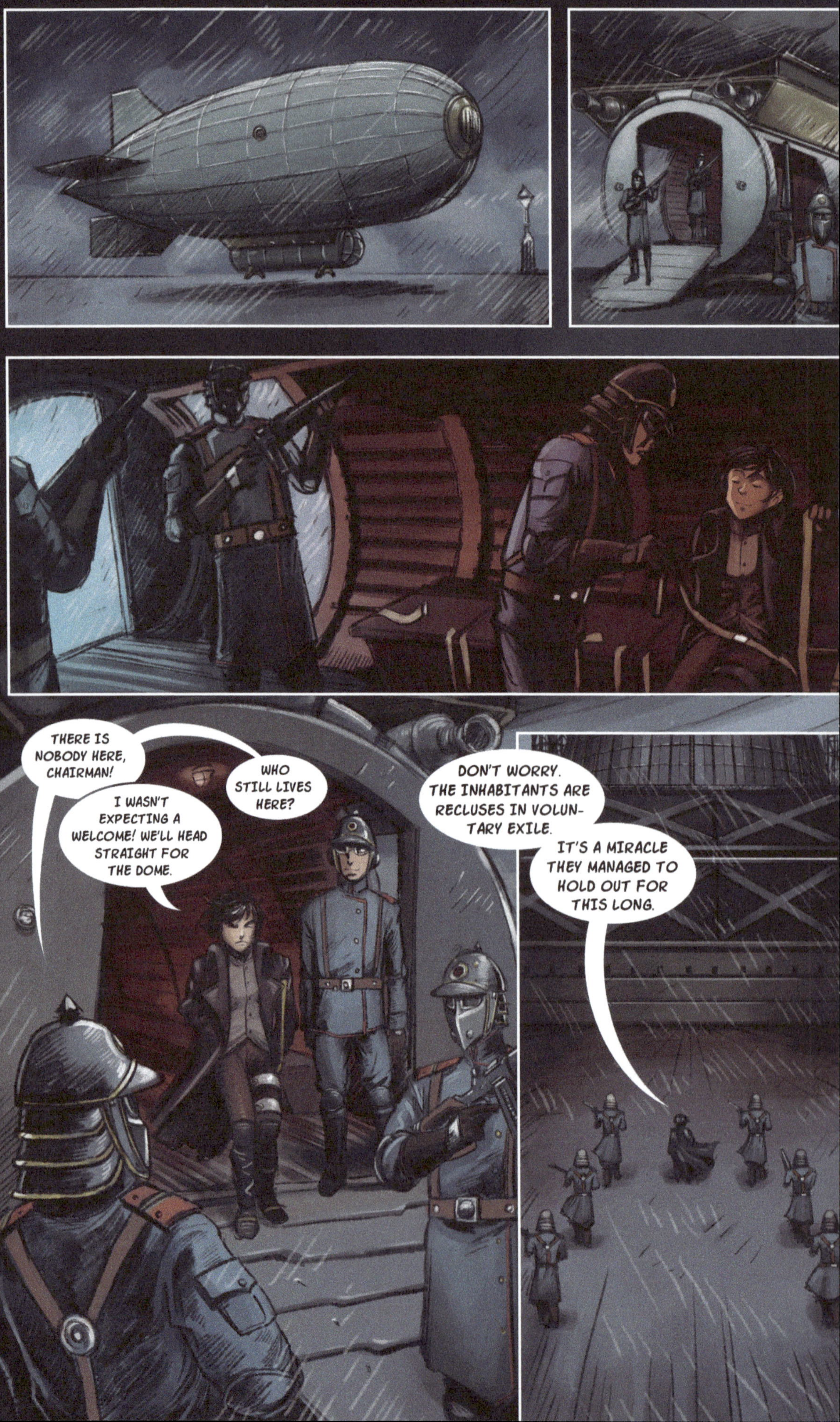

IS THAT WHAT I THINK IT IS
A COMET ROCKET. MY LITTLE BROTHER USED TO PLAY WITH MODELS OF THAT THING.
I ONCE HEARD THEY BUILT ANOTHER. GUESS NOBODY DARED TO FLY IT AFTER THOSE FIRST TWO DISASTERS.

DING!
BONJOUR, MADAME!
MIND IF I COME IN? THIS COLD IS WREAKING HAVOC ON MY CONSTITUTION.

YOU MUST BE FROM THE ASSOCIATION, MY GRANDFA-THER WAS VERY CLEAR IN HIS RESPONSE.
AND WE WERE VERY CLEAR THAT HE DIDN'T HAVE A CHOICE.
NOW, CONSIDERING THE FACT YOU DIDN'T USE THAT GUN EMPLACEMENT BY THE LANDING PAD, YOU ARE ALONE?
MY GRANDFATHER IS OLD. THERE IS LITTLE YOU CAN THREATEN HIM WITH.
THREATEN? OH, NON, MADAME. VOUS AVEZ MAL COMPRIS. I AM HERE TO MAKE HIM AN OFFER.
HE'S NOT INTERESTED.
TELL ME, IS YOUR GRAND PAPA UNABLE TO SPEAK FOR HIMSELF?
HE IS FINE.

BIENE. I'LL GO SEE HIM THEN.

NO.

I'VE HAD ENOUGH OF THIS... MOVE HER OUT OF THE WAY.

DO YOU HAVE ANY STAFF MADAME?
SOME. . . THEY ARE AWAY, FETCHING SUPPLIES.
THEY TOOK THE ONLY BOAT?
YES.

INTÉRESSANTE...

IS THAT ELEVATOR STILL WORKING?
IT'S HARD FOR ME TO WALK SUCH STAIRS.

TAP!

MR. GHULAM ALI, JE SUPPOSE?
ARE YOU MOCKING ME, MADEMOISELLE?

YOU WILL ADDRESS ME AS CHAIRMAN.
YOU CAME INTO OUR HOME WITH ARMED THUGS. I'LL ADDRESS YOU THE WAY I LIKE, GIRL.

I AM SORRY, BUT YOU FORCED MY HAND. YOU HAVE SOMETHING I DESIRE.

OH, JE COMPRENDS . . .

ALL I HAVE TO DO IS PUSH THIS DETONATOR...
AND THE PAYLOAD INSIDE THE COMET III WILL EXPLODE.

YOU'RE DETERMINED.
YOU THINK HUMANITY CAN'T REACH THE STARS WITHOUT YOUR HELP?
UTTER-KRAPP LAUNCHED ITS FIRST PROTOTYPE A FEW MONTHS AGO.
THOSE IDIOTS COULDN'T REACH THE CLOUDS.
I WORKED MY WHOLE LIFE TO GET A ROCKET TO ELYSIUM. IT'S ONLY FAIR IT DIES WITH ME.
THEY REACHED THE STRATO-SPHERE.
!!!
THAT'S RIGHT... WHILE YOU HAVE BEEN LIVING IN THIS SNOWGLOBE, WITH YOUR MEMORIES OF FADED FAME, HUMANITY HAS PROGRESSED WITHOUT YOU.
WELL, IF YOU ARE SO WELL OFF WITHOUT ME, WHY ARE YOU HERE?
WHAT CAN YOU POSSIBLY OFFER ME?
URGENCY. YOU HAVE WHAT WE NEED, AND WE CAN GIVE YOU WHAT YOU WANT.
WE KNOW YOUR SUPPORTERS ARE STILL TRYING TO ACQUIRE THE FUNDING FOR THE LAUNCH OF THE COMET III. WE CAN PROVIDE.

I'M SERIOUS, MONSIEUR.
I CAN BRING YOU BACK INTO THE PUBLIC CONSCIOUSNESS SO YOUR NAME WILL NEVER BE ASSOCIATED WITH FAILURE AGAIN.

CURIOSITY L...
TO THE STA...

WHY WOULD I BELIEVE YOU?

REMEMBER WHAT NAPOLEON SAID WHEN YOU WERE ADMITTED TO THE ACADEMY D'AÉRONAUTIQUE?
IF YOU NEVER SPREAD YOUR WINGS, YOU'LL NEVER KNOW HOW FAR YOU CAN FLY.

HOW DO YOU KNOW THAT ?!

NEVER MIND THAT, MON AMI . . .
DO YOU WANT THE COMET TO REACH ELYSIUM?

WHETHER YOU BENEFIT OR NOT IS IRRELEVANT TO ME. EVERYONE KNOWS YOU WANT TO MAKE HISTORY.
I AM OFFERING YOU THAT CHANCE. YOU ALREADY SACRIFICED SO MUCH. WHAT DOES YOUR PRIDE MEAN TO YOU AT THIS POINT?

I GET WHAT I WANT, WITH OR WITHOUT YOU.

IT'S ALL I HAVE LEFT.

THINK OF WHAT YOU GET IN RETURN...
ONE LAST CHANCE AT FLYING!

GIVE IT
TO ME.

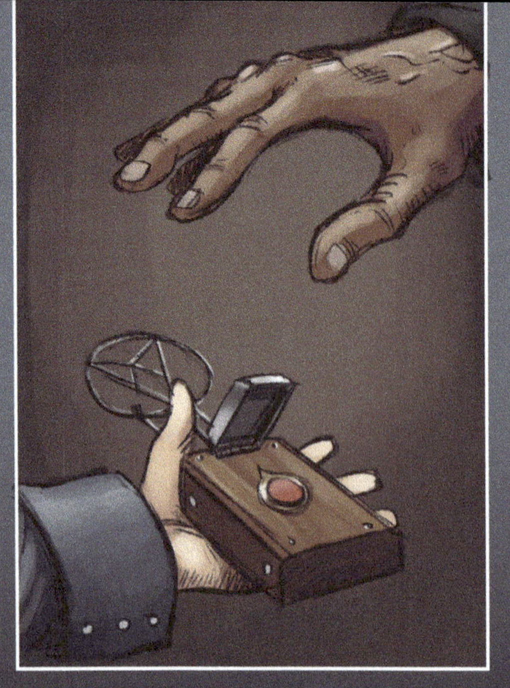

THUD

CRACK!

AN HOUR LATER...
CHAIRMAN, CAN I HAVE A WORD?
AFFIRMATIVE...
WE'RE GOING TO KEEP AN EYE ON THAT ONE.
OUI.

IS THAT MAN, GHULAM ALI?
OUI.

THAT MAN DEVELOPED THE ROCKETS WITH WHICH NAPOLEON BOMBED MY GRANDPARENTS!

THE PAST IS THE PAST. WE CAN ONLY JUDGE HIM FOR HIS PRESENT ACTIONS. AND HE AGREED TO HELP.
WHAT?!
IT MEANS WE ARE GOING TO EXPLORE ELYSIUM, TU COMPRENDS?
HE WORKED FOR NAPOLEON.
YOU THINK HE CAN BE TRUSTED ?
AS MUCH AS HE CAN TRUST US.
WE ARE HIS LAST CHANCE AT FULFILLING HIS DREAM.
AND THAT LAUNCH MIGHT BE OUR LAST CHANCE AT DOING ANYTHING AT ALL.

Ghulam Ali
(Subject-17)

Ghulam Ali (Subject 17) was born a cousin to the late Tipi Sultan of Mysore (1750-1799). He fled India for France after the British conquered Mysore in 1799. In 1804, he secured employment with the Academy d'Aeronautica, where he was heading the development of the R-2 rockets used to attack England during the Napoleonic Wars. After

coalition forces entered Paris in 1812, he escaped prosecution only to reappear years later in New York to announce his plans for the Babylon Foundation. Thanks to patronage from the similarly-minded elite, his organization repurposed an oil platform in the Atlantic Ocean used to launch manned rockets to Elysium. However, after the disastrous launch attempts of Comet I (1821) and the mysterious disappearance of the Comet II (1824), Ghulam fell out of favor. He has been living on the Babylon platform ever since, fading from public awareness.

In light of recent events, however, the Chair believes the time has come to revitalize Project Icarus.

The 7th Chairman
(Subject-09)

After evaluation by various physicians, it was decided S-09 could take on a position of responsibility. She was given an honorary appointment to the Chair in an advisory role.

S-09 first request was to have her Subject-status nullified. This request was denied.

A year later, it was believed she had shown enough competence to elevate her status to that of a regular Chairman. The motion got passed with a 5-to-3 vote. However, she wouldn't be allowed to give orders directly without the approval of a fellow Chairman.

She requested her subject status be revoked- again. This was denied- again. Hereby we request to restrict access to her case file as a precaution.

I SEE. WHAT AN INTERESTING CHARACTER.
INTERESTING IS AN UNDER-STATEMENT.
HE DEVELOPED WEAPONS FOR THE EMPEROR JUST TO REALIZE HIS AMBITIONS.
THAT IS WHY PEOPLE RATHER REMEMBER MEN LIKE DR. ALI FOR THEIR HIS-TORICAL CONTRIBUTIONS THAN FOR THEIR CHARACTER, CORPORAL.
HOW ABOUT YOU?
EXCUSE ME?
WHAT ARE YOU WILLING TO DO FOR A PLACE IN THE HISTORY BOOKS ?
I JUST WANTED TO SERVE.
OH, SUCH HUMILITY. SURELY YOU HAVE GOALS.
I PREFER TO TAKE THINGS A STEP AT A TIME.
I SEE. IN THAT CASE. . . I HOPE YOU TAUGHT YOURSELF TO JUMP AHEAD FROM TIME TO TIME, CORPORAL.

BECAUSE
WE ARE ABOUT TO
MAKE ONE HELL
OF A LEAP.

to be Continued....

National Republican.

Vol. I. WASHINGTON, D. C., MONDAY, MARCH 4, 1821. No. 81.

Mankind's first launch into space ends in a Ball of Flames

"Oh, the Humanity!" I heard a reporter scream into his microphone as an astounded audience looked at the burning ruble that was supposed to be, not only the awnser to humanities oldest ambitions, but it greatest achivement. Onlookers counted down expecting a momement of triumph, but when they cried: "Zero", The Comet exploded killing all souls onboard.

The day the people of all nations were anticipating ended in tragedy. From all around the civilised world there are stories of people who woke up behind their radio sets (they bought just to be a witness of this event) convinced they woke up from a nightmare. Many friends admitted to me they cheered as the heard the roaring voilence, assuming it were the engines igniting, but a las. The Babylon personnel barely managed to contain the fires and many visitors jumped of f the platform in a panic into the water below. I and other onlookers had to volunteer to save these poor people from the ocean as the staff was to busy getting the fire under control. Fortenatlely 'we' were successful in saving everyone, but the crew who dedicated their lifes to this mission.

The Comet did not leave the Babylon Launch Platform. The rocket was supposed to launch 8 am local time, enter earth's gravitational field and pass the Elysium-Object three times to take photo's up close and return. The crew of six was supposed to land in a capsule hanging from a parachute as the US navy would pick them up and return the cosmonauts the neutral Babylon Platform in the middle of the Pacific Ocean. All

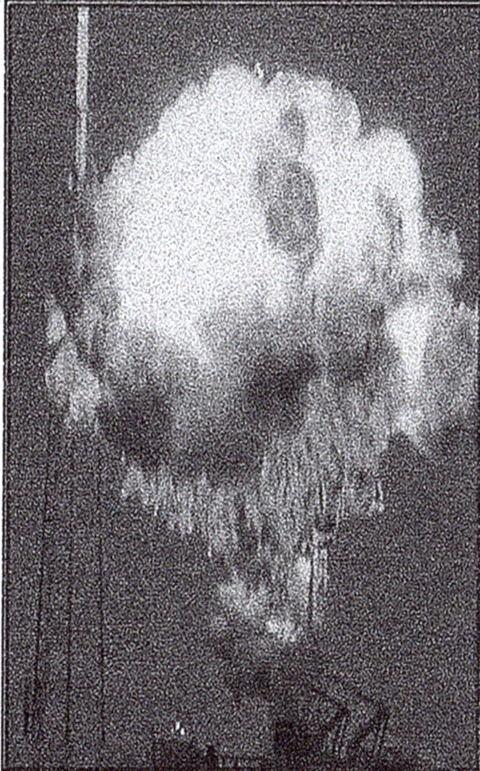

this planning was naught. Now everyone is asking how this could have happend? As of yet, there are no answers. The head of the project Ghulam Ali is under fire, as the designer of the Comet, who is not known to take critism well. And his opponents have also taken this time to, once again, remind the public he developed AR-1 explosive rocket that terrorised the coast of Britain during the reign of Napoleon.

Is this the end of the Babylon Project?

Ali Says: "No!"

Prof. Ali proclaimed the Babylon Project can prepare the next launch within a couple of years, while they get to the bottom of the incident. World leaders have offered they condolences to the families who lost loved ones and have proposed to establish a independent committe to investigate the cause of the accident. "It's a thinly veiled attempt to spy on our efforts", Ali claimed. Meanwhile senator Walker stated in congress yesterday. "There has been a severe lack of oversight on the taxpayers expense and these brave cosmonauts paid the price." No goverents or sponsors have come forward on their decision to continue supporting the project.

The crew of The Comet who gave their lives for this mission from top left to bottom right.

Thomas Daily (Cpt.), Maria Estaphan (Computor),
Lerom Jurkins (Pilot), Georgy Remek (Pilot),
Jule Cameron (Photographer), Jan Yurchikhin (Physicist)

FREE PRESS.

No. 8.   HALIFAX, N. C. FRIDAY, MAY 14, 1824.   VOL I.

UTTER-KRAPP IS SHOOTING FOR THE STARS

"We'll have men on the moon by 1830" Utter-Krapp spokesperson Miss Spelling declared. In the wake of the failed second attempt to launch a manned vehicle to Elysium it looks like the Babylon Project is about to collapse. Several investors have already announced retracting their funding and there are rumors of Ghulum Ali being sued for matters of deception, negligence and fraud.

What happened to The Comet II and who is responsible is still a matter of discussion. But the competition doesn't waste any time taking on Ali's former employees who are leaving the launch platform where they constructed the Comet rockets. "The conditions were getting unacceptable , but we kept working. We wanted to keep supporting each other," Jan-Kees the Bruin explained . "We wanted to redeem ourselves for what happened the first time. But now, we had to say, enough is enough." Mister de Bruin is one the many Members that found new employment after the Comet II incident. "It feels like a second chance. The goal is the same, just the target is different... Now we have a new team and a fresh set of eyes. It might have been the thing we needed in the first place." We found the same sentiment along other former staff members. "We want to apply the knowledge gained in more fields than space travel," miss Spelling proclaimed. "We are talking rocket proppeled blimps, coaches and to replace the pony express while we are at it." Regardless of their other ambitions, Utter-Krapp has announced their space program includes landing cosmonauts on the moon and developing means to create a permanent presence there.

on May 3rd, After the much anticipated launch, The Comet II disappeared from sight just when it left earth orbit as it approached Elysium. "As far as we can tell it just vanished." Mister Burke, a member of the astronomical society says. "We tracked the rocket's flight very closely with our telescopes and suddenly it was gone and it's smoke trail just ended... No explosion of falling debris." After weeks of investigation, there is still no answer The conspiracy savy have suggested it might actually have been "smoke and mirrors" and some parties have created models on how the Babylon Project used actual magician tricks the create the illusion of a rocket launch. Ridiculous? Experts responded to these reports with: "It is as good an explanation as any other."

This photo was taken right after the Comet II disappeared from sight.

Babylon will not prevail

As credibility diminishes funding is being pulled from the project. "The whole thing has been a waste of money." MP Watts-Russell stated in an interview. It was an investment in one man's dream that wouldn't have payed even if it succeeded." Parlement decided to suspend further funding.
"Monsiour Ali has a lot to explain." The MP continued. "He should also be held to account for his action during the war and his crmies against the British people."
It seems accusers and angry investors are closing in on the entrepeneur, who hasn't made any public appearances since the 1st of May. Meanwhile, companies like Utter Krapp are picking up the pieces a former staff members are lookin for new employment. What else can we conclude other than Babylon will not prevail.

WHO'S ABSENT?
Is it You?